For anyone who feels like they don't belong
— C. S. & O. B.

For Sue, Gwen, Harlow, and Rue
— M. C.

A Feiwel and Friends Book
An imprint of Macmillan Publishing Group, LLC
120 Broadway, New York, NY 10271
mackids.com

Our books may be purchased in bulk for promotional, educational, or business use.
Please contact your local bookseller or the Macmillan Corporate and Premium Sales Department
at (800) 221-7945 ext. 5442 or by email at MacmillanSpecialMarkets@macmillan.com.

Library of Congress Cataloging-in-Publication Data is available.

First edition, 2023
Book design by Sharismar Rodriguez
Feiwel and Friends logo designed by Filomena Tuosto
Printed in the United States of America by Worzalla, Stevens Point, Wisconsin

ISBN 978-1-250-35172-2
1 3 5 7 9 10 8 6 4 2

COROOK & OLIVIA BARTON

If I Were a Fish

ART BY
MIKE CURATO

FEIWEL AND FRIENDS
NEW YORK

If I were a fish

and you caught me . . .

Shimmering in the sun,

Such a rare one . . .

Can't believe that
You caught one!

If I were a fish and you caught me,
You'd say "Look at that fish,"
Heaviest in the sea . . .

You'd win first prize
If you caught me!

Why's everybody on the internet so mean?
Why's everybody so afraid of what they've never seen?

If I was scrolling through and I saw me
Flopping around and singing my song,
I'd say "Wow, they're cute"
And sing along!

Happiest as a pair . . .

I found you—now I'm not scared!

Why's everybody on the internet so mean?
Why's everybody so afraid of what they've never seen?

If I was scrolling through and I saw me
Flopping around and singing my song,
I'd say "Wow, they're cute" and sing along!

How lucky are we?

Of all the fish in the sea?

You get to be you

and I get to be me.